W9-CAZ-493

© & TM 2016 Lucasfilm Ltd. All rights reserved.
Published by Disney • Lucasfilm Press, an imprint of Disney Book Group. No part of
this book may be reproduced or transmitted in any form or by any means, electronic
or mechanical, including photocopying, recording, or by any information storage and
retrieval system, without written permission from the publisher.

For information address Disney • Lucasfilm Press,
1101 Flower Street, Glendale, California 91201.

Printed in China
First Hardcover Edition, July 2016   10 9 8 7 6 5 4 3 2 1

ISBN 978-1-4847-8699-4
FAC-023680-16195

Visit the official *Star Wars* website at: www.starwars.com
This book was printed on paper created from a sustainable source.

STAR WARS®

Rescue from Jabba's Palace

Book Nine

Disney | LUCASFILM
PRESS
Los Angeles • New York

C

-3PO and R2-D2 were back on Tatooine. The droids had been sent to the desert planet by Luke Skywalker on a mission to deliver a special message to the gangster Jabba the Hutt. At Jabba's palace, C-3PO introduced himself and R2-D2 to Jabba's servant Bib Fortuna. Then they were escorted into Jabba's court.

Jabba the Hutt was enormous slimy alien. His court was filled with a variety of creatures from all over the galaxy. Being surrounded by so many rough-looking creatures made C-3PO nervous, but R2-D2 immediately began Luke's message. In a hologram, Luke Skywalker tried to bargain for Han Solo's life. He offered Jabba a gift in return: the two droids!

C-3PO was shocked, but Jabba just laughed. He was not about to give up Han Solo, who hung on his wall frozen in a block of carbonite. But he would keep the droids anyway!

Jabba was pleased with how many languages C-3PO could speak. He assigned the protocol droid to be a translator inside his court and sent R2-D2 to work on his sail barge. C-3PO was surprised when a masked bounty hunter later arrived with Chewbacca, Han Solo's Wookiee companion. Jabba bought Chewbacca from the bounty hunter, then threw Chewie into a cell.

One of Jabba's guards looked on with interest. He was really Han's friend Lando Calrissian in disguise. . . .

Hours later, the masked bounty hunter snuck back into the now-empty hall. The hunter began to free Han from his frozen tomb. Soon the carbonite melted and Han fell to the floor.

Han couldn't see, but the bounty hunter told him that his eyesight would soon return. Then Han's mysterious rescuer removed the helmet it was wearing. It was Princess Leia!

But before Leia and Han could escape, they were captured by Jabba's guards.

The next morning, a cloaked figured entered Jabba's palace. It was Luke Skywalker, dressed as a Jedi Knight!

Bib Fortuna told Luke that Jabba would not see him. But Luke used an old Jedi mind trick to make Bib Fortuna take him to Jabba.

Luke arrived in Jabba's court and nodded to Princess Leia, who was now chained to Jabba as his slave.

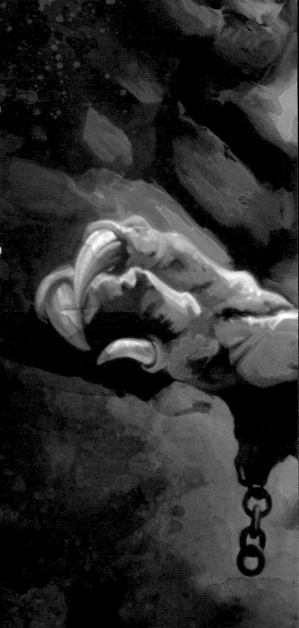

Jabba knew that Luke had tricked Bib Fortuna into letting him in. "Your mind powers will not work on me, boy," Jabba began. "I shall enjoy watching you die."

Jabba laughed, then flipped a switch, causing Luke to fall through a trapdoor into a pit below.

There, an enormous gate opened to release a huge snarling monster—a rancor! The beast quickly turned its attention to the young Jedi, who steered it back toward the gate.

As the rancor moved in for the kill, Luke grabbed a skull from the floor and hurled it at a control panel. It was a direct hit. The gate crashed back down, squashing the giant creature!

Jabba was infuriated. He ordered Luke, Han, and Chewie to be brought to him at once. "They will all suffer for this outrage," the gangster grunted.

Jabba—with Leia still chained to him—boarded his flying sail barge while his prisoners were forced onto a flying skiff. Luke and his friends would be thrown into a pit, where a monster called the Sarlacc would eat them alive!

When the skiff reached the pit, one of Jabba's guards pushed Luke onto a plank that extended high over the creature's mouth. Without warning, Luke jumped, grabbed the end of the plank, and catapulted himself into the air!

At the same time, R2-D2, still working on Jabba's barge, launched Luke's lightsaber—which had been hidden inside the droid the whole time—into the Jedi's waiting hand! Luke ignited the saber and quickly went on the attack.

Jabba's men fought back, and Lando fell off the skiff! Han and Chewie sprang into action and rescued their friend before the Sarlacc could finish him off.

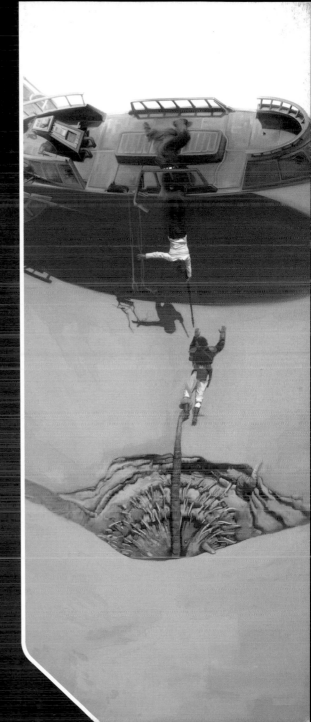

Back on the sail barge, Leia took advantage of the commotion and attacked Jabba the Hutt while he was distracted.

She threw her chain around Jabba's neck and pulled as hard as she could. Thanks to Leia, Jabba would never enslave anyone else again.

A few minutes later, R2-D2 arrived in Jabba's chamber. The little droid fired a small laser, breaking the chain that kept Leia from escaping. Together, they found C-3PO and raced to the barge's upper deck to help their friends.

On the upper deck, Luke Skywalker was busy deflecting blaster fire with his lightsaber. He was just fighting off the last of Jabba's men when Princess Leia arrived.

Luke told Leia to point the barge's cannon at the deck. They were going to blow up the sail barge!

R2-D2 pushed
C-3PO off the ship
and then followed him
to safety on the ground
below.

Once Luke was sure
that the droids were okay,
he grabbed a rigging rope
in one arm and Leia in
the other. Then the young
Jedi kicked the trigger
and the cannon blasted the
deck. Luke and Leia swung
toward the skiff as the cannon
continued to fire.

Luke and Leia landed on the skiff beside Han and Chewie.

"Don't forget the droids!" Luke yelled to his friends.

Lando, who was at the controls, immediately steered the skiff away from the sail barge toward the droids.

The friends found the droids stuck in the sand and used the skiff's magnets to pull them on board. Then Lando punched the controls, and the skiff flew across the desert. Behind them, Jabba's sail barge collapsed in a final fiery explosion!

As the heroes left the desert planet in separate ships, Han called Luke over the X-wing's comm. "Thanks for coming after me," he said to the young Jedi. "I owe you one."

With Han rescued and Jabba the Hutt defeated, the heroes rocketed away from Tatooine for the last time. They were ready to take on an even bigger challenge—Darth Vader!